PETER SHERIDAN

BULLET AND THE ARK

Peter Sheridan is one of Ireland's best-known figures in theatre. He co-founded and ran the Project Theatre Company. His best-selling book *44: A Dublin Memoir* was published to wide acclaim in 1999, followed by *Forty-Seven Roses* (2001) and *Big Fat Love* (2003). He has also written *Old Money, New Money* for the Open Door series.

NEW ISLAND *Open Door*

BULLET AND THE ARK
First published 2008
by New Island
2 Brookside
Dundrum Road
Dublin 14

www.newisland.ie

A CIP catalogue record for this book is available from the British
Library.

ISBN 978-1-905494-84-2

New Island receives financial assistance from
The Arts Council (An Chomhairle Ealaíon), Dublin, Ireland.

Printed in Ireland by ColourBooks
Cover design by Artmark

1 3 5 4 2

Dear Reader,

On behalf of myself and the other contributing authors, I would like to welcome you to the sixth Open Door series. We hope that you enjoy the books and that reading becomes a lasting pleasure in your life.

Warmest wishes,

Patricia Scanlan.

Patricia Scanlan
Series Editor

For Xabi, my grandson –
you've brought so much joy into my life.

The inspiration for this book came from a conversation
with Terry Fagan of the North Inner City Folklore
Project. Without that spark, the story as it is here
would never have seen the light of day.
My gratitude to you now and always, Terry.

One

Bullet Ferguson loved animals. He thought they were nicer than humans. He could never imagine fighting with a rabbit or a pet mouse or anything with fluffy fur. They were so warm to the touch. He loved it when they wriggled in his hand. He laughed when he put his finger in a guinea pig's mouth and it nibbled him. He squealed with delight when a hamster ran up his sleeve and came out at his neck.

Bullet loved Champ above every other animal in the world. Champ was a black terrier dog. His name was short for Champion. His ears were funny and he only had one eye. One of his ears pointed straight up in the air. The other one pointed straight out to the side. They never changed position, even when he ran. One of the kids in the area called him 'Three O'Clock' because that was the time by his ears. The name stuck and everyone called Champ Three O'Clock. Bullet, on the other hand, only ever called him Champ. He chased kids up streets and down alleys if they called Champ names. As a result, he became a brilliant runner. And that's how he got the name Bullet.

The cat who plucked Champ's eye out was called Princess. She belonged to Mr Barrett. He lived in the flat next door. Princess was a white cat and she was vicious. Any time Champ came near, she hunched her back and flashed her teeth.

'Do you want me to kill her?' Bullet asked Champ after he had been attacked. Bullet had to defend his dog.

'I don't want you to hurt her,' Champ told him.

Bullet was surprised because Champ could be vicious too when it suited him.

'I can set a trap for her,' Bullet said. 'You don't have to get involved.'

'No, it's bad enough humans killing one another without us starting,' said Champ.

'I'm your master and I have to stand up for you,' Bullet replied.

'I understand that, but it's not your fight.'

★

Champ used to sleep alone in the kitchen, by the back door. One night,

Bullet heard him and knew that he was having dog nightmares. He went down to him and lay with him until he settled. He put his head against Champ and listened to his breathing. It was faster than his own. So he speeded up his breathing to match Champ's. He was so close that he could feel Champ's breath on his face. There was a real doggy flavour to it. Their breathing fell into a rhythm.

That night, Champ was the first to speak. 'I can hear your heart,' he said.

'Did you just speak?' Bullet had asked.

'Yes, I did. I can stop if you want me to.'

'No, no, don't stop. It's just that I never heard a dog talk before.'

'That's because you never listened.'

'Really?'

'Yeah. No one listens. Why do you think we bark all the time?'

'Is it to get attention?'

'You got it in one!'

That was how it started. Bullet brought Champ's mattress up to his room. He let him sleep at the side of his bed. Now they could talk all night if they wanted to. And sometimes they did.

Bullet didn't talk to his father. There was no point in talking to someone whose two favourite words were 'shut' and 'up'. He could have talked to his mother, but she had left over a year ago. He remembered her smell better than her face. He had a photograph hidden away from his father. He looked at it from time to time so as not to forget what she looked like. One day she put on her hat and coat and disappeared out the door. She got tired of being told to shut up and vanished. Bullet missed her, but he had Champ.

★

'Do I have a stupid face?' Champ asked him one night.

'You have a beautiful face,' Bullet said. 'What makes you think it's stupid?'

'I don't look like a dog. I look like a clock.'

'That's not true.'

'It is true. Stop trying to protect me.'

'Sticks and stones may break my bones, but names will never hurt me,' Bullet sang out.

It was an old saying, but it was also a lie. Names did hurt. Worse than knives, sometimes. Bullet now understood that animals were sensitive, too. No one was going to call his dog Three O'Clock and get away with it.

Two

Dizzy and Oxo were in charge of
finding the wood to make the boat.
Bullet was in charge of designing it.
They came up with the idea when they
were messing in town one day. They
were crossing the Matt Talbot Bridge
when they saw a tall ship with a big
white sail.

Bullet stopped and stared at it like
he had had a vision.

'There it is,' he said. 'I'm going to
build a ship.'

The boys were dreamers. They
made plans all the time and nothing

7

came of them. The ship was different. It was simple. Wood floated on water. You didn't have to do anything with it. A few planks stuck together and you had something. A white sheet for a sail and you didn't need an engine. The wind was your power and it was free. Simple, like all great ideas.

Bullet gave his instructions like any good captain would.

'You get the wood, Dizzy,' he said. 'And don't fall asleep on the job.'

It was a dig at Dizzy because of the time he fainted in school and they couldn't wake him up. He had fainted on purpose. Most schoolboys knew that if you put blotting paper in your shoes it was supposed to make you light-headed. When they took off Dizzy's shoes and socks they found loads of blotting paper. The teacher himself nearly fainted with the stink off it. Dizzy had been wearing the blotting paper for two weeks non-stop. It was stuck to his skin like superglue. He had to go to hospital to have it removed. When he came back to school a week later, everyone called him Dizzy. And, just like the blotting paper, it stuck.

'I only fainted once in my life, I'll have you know,' Dizzy barked back at Bullet, slightly hurt.

'It doesn't mean you won't faint again,' Oxo said, smiling from ear to ear. He loved slagging Dizzy, especially when he had Bullet's approval.

'Where am I going to get the wood to build a ship?' Dizzy asked.

'You're going to beg, borrow and steal it,' Bullet replied.

'What's my job going to be?' Oxo asked. 'Can I take charge of getting the food?'

Food was Oxo's favourite subject. He always thought about his belly first and everything else second. Oxo loved everything that went into his mouth. He had yet to discover a food he didn't love. One day, for a dare, he crumbled an Oxo cube and ate it without taking any water. He was known as Oxo after that.

'You are going to get the sail,' Bullet told him.

'Where am I going to get the sail?' Oxo said.

'You're going to get it off your old fella's bed,' Bullet said.

'My old fella doesn't have a sheet. He sleeps on the couch most nights.'

'Then rob it off a clothesline when no one is watching,' Bullet said.

It was an idea that silenced Oxo, a rare event. Bullet looked back to the tall ship bobbing on the river. A lot of planks made up that ship, he thought. And a lot of sheets, too. It would take them a million years to gather up the wood for a ship that size. Maybe they should be thinking about a boat instead. A boat was only half the size of a ship.

They split up and went looking in different parts of the city. Oxo saw three yellow sheets in a garden. He hopped the wall and grabbed them.

The boys had arranged to meet at four o'clock. Oxo turned up with the sheets. Bullet had a copybook with a drawing of a boat. Dizzy had a hammer and a bag of nails but no wood.

'All we have is a sail,' Oxo said. 'That's stupid.'

'I have an uncle,' Dizzy said.

'I have four uncles,' Bullet said.

'I have three uncles and two aunties,' Oxo said.

'I have only one uncle and guess what? He's the foreman in a wood factory,' Dizzy said.

Dizzy's Uncle Pat worked in the yard of a cash and carry. He wasn't the foreman, but he drove a forklift storing wooden pallets. There were hundreds of them, piled up against a twenty-foot wall. He told the boys they could take as many as they liked so long as they didn't burn them in a bonfire. Bullet opened the copybook and showed Pat the drawing of the boat, just like the one on the Liffey.

'I'm going to have to change my design,' he said.

'That's very good. Are you studying art in school?' Pat asked him.

'No, I'm not. I don't go to school. I mitch all the time,' Bullet said.

'We hate school,' Oxo said.

'I don't hate school. I might go back to school in September,' Dizzy said.

Bullet and Oxo knew he was only sucking up to his uncle, but they said nothing. They were getting the pallets for free. That was more important. It also involved a change of plan. A boat was out of the question now. The best they could do was nail some of the pallets together.

'We're not going to build a boat,' Bullet said. 'We're going to build a raft instead.'

Oxo and Dizzy thought it was a great idea. A raft was just a floating platform. They had the raw materials. All they needed to do was stick them together. They could even do that with ropes. A wooden barrel in each of the four corners would finish the job off perfectly. Bullet got busy making a new drawing with all the changes. Then Oxo said they could turn the whole thing into an ark.

'How could we do that?' Dizzy asked.

'We could put some animals on it,' Oxo said. 'The same as Noah.'

'Do you mean like Bullet's dog, Th——'

It almost slipped out. Dizzy was on the point of saying Three O'Clock when he pulled himself back. But Bullet was busy with the new design. When he realised they were talking about an ark, he thought it was the best idea they had ever had.

Three

That night, Bullet told Champ the plan. He made it sound like it was his idea from start to finish. Champ didn't seem too impressed.

'I don't really like boats,' Champ said.

'It's not a boat. We're building an ark.'

'It might make me seasick.'

'You can jump into the water and swim. You like swimming, don't you?'

'Sometimes.'

'I'll jump in beside you and give you a race.'

'Whatever.'

Bullet hated that word. It was cheeky. He felt like giving Champ a slap on the nose. But he would never hit him. It was better to talk things out. He knew from his father that violence didn't work. Whenever his father gave him a dig, Bullet went back into his shell. In his mind, he stuck knives into his father's chest and watched him bleed to death. He put a plastic bag over his head and smiled at him gasping for air. He put rat poison in the sugar bowl and sniggered at him stirring it into his tea. He could hold onto feelings like that for days and weeks. He could murder his father, but it wouldn't bring his mother back.

He didn't want Champ having those feelings for him. The dog was his best friend. He never wanted that to change. He would rather cut off his arm than strike him. And he didn't feel that way for Champ alone. Bullet felt that towards all of the animal kingdom.

He asked Champ what was upsetting him. But Champ wouldn't answer. Bullet tickled him under the chin, but there was no response. Bullet went to the press in the kitchen and came back with two dog biscuits. Champ sat up and stuck his tongue out. Bullet kept the biscuits behind his back.

'I want to know what's bothering you,' Bullet said.

'Biscuit first,' Champ replied.

'No, biscuit second.'

'Biscuit first and I'll tell you, I promise.'

'Sorry,' Bullet said. He put the biscuits in his pocket.

Champ started to drool. Champ was a clever dog. But when food was around, his brains disappeared.

'I don't like cats, that's all,' Champ said.

'I know you don't like cats. Tell me something new,' Bullet said.

'I don't want to go on the ark if there are cats on it.'

The penny dropped for Bullet. He realised this was about Princess, the white cat who had reduced Champ to just one eye. Of course he didn't want to go on a cruise with her. Bullet took out the two biscuits and gave them to Champ.

'Princess won't be coming with us. She's dead,' he said.

The truth was she was very much alive. She had gone down the country with her owner, Mr Barrett, to his brother in Cork. He had lots of mice and needed to get rid of them. As soon as Princess had done her work on the mice of Cork, she would be back in her usual haunts in the north inner city of Dublin. For the moment, however, she was out of sight. Bullet wanted to keep her out of mind, too.

Champ ate the biscuits. He licked Bullet on the calf of each leg. It was something he did every time he was fed. Bullet loved the feeling of Champ's wet tongue on his skin.

That night, they talked about the ark. Champ knew much more about the history of it than Bullet. Every animal had grown up on tales of how they had survived the great flood. Bullet had heard of Noah. But he did not know that it had rained non-stop for forty days and forty nights. Everyone in the world had drowned except for those in the boat. If God hadn't told Noah to bring two of everything, the world would have come to an end. If man didn't turn away from sin, God might not give warnings the next time.

Bullet was scared out of his wits. Why hadn't he paid attention in school when he had had the chance? It was almost too late. There had been a great wave somewhere in Asia and thousands had drowned. It was called a tsunami. What if one of them was to come down the Liffey and swallow Dublin? Only the people on top of big buildings, and the smart people who had their own boats, would survive.

Champ wasn't too worried about tsunamis. Champ was more worried about who was going to be with him on the ark. Noah had brought two of everything, a male and a female. So who was Bullet going to pair him with?

'Have you considered a companion for me?' Champ asked.

'I don't know what you mean,' Bullet replied.

'Have you got a bitch in mind for me on the ark?'

'No, I don't have a bitch in mind.'

'I don't want anything big or hairy. Something small, with a gentle nature.'

'What about a poodle?'

'No, I don't like curls. A Jack Russell might be nice.'

Champ then put his paw across his good eye. He did this when he was embarrassed or shy. Bullet saw it straight away.

'There will be no bitch for you on the ark,' Bullet said. 'You're coming on your own.'

Champ was glad. He preferred when it was just him and his master. He didn't want a third party getting in the way.

Four

Oxo borrowed a pram. Then the boys collected the pallets from Dizzy's Uncle Pat. Three at a time was all they could manage. They got the first load back to the courtyard of the flats. Bullet stayed with them while the other two went back for more. While he was minding the pallets, Bullet made a new design in the copybook. Four pallets made a nice square, but it was a bit small. Six made a funny shape. He didn't like it. Eight was even worse. But nine was lovely. Three by three by three, a lucky

number and a lovely, perfect square.
Bullet showed it to the boys when they
got back with the second load.

The boys went back once more.
While they were gone, Bullet made lists
of things that they needed for the task
ahead: paint, varnish, brushes, cloths,
white spirits, rollers, gloves, ropes.
Bullet went up to his flat and collected
Champ. He tied him to one of the
pallets.

'You're to mind this, Champ. Attack
anyone who tries to rob it,' Bullet told
him.

'You're mad the way you talk to that
dog,' Oxo said.

'That dog can't understand you,'
Dizzy added.

Bullet turned from Champ and
looked at them.

'I'm his master. He's my servant.'

Champ barked twice in agreement.
Champ never spoke when there were

others around. That was just for when they were alone.

'Try and rob one of the pallets,' Bullet told his friends.

They didn't want to. Champ was only a little terrier, but the one eye had a mean, vicious look. He was, in truth, a teddy bear with an ugly face.

'I'll try and nick one,' Bullet said.

He reached out to touch a pallet. Before his hand got there, Champ exploded into a frenzy of barking. He leapt in the air and almost bit Bullet's hand off.

'I think the pallets are safe,' Bullet said.

The boys headed off and knocked at every door in the neighbourhood looking for supplies. They got brushes that were a hundred years old and some with bristles that were stuck together. At one house they got a sweeping brush. It was of no use, but they kept it anyway. They got tins of paint that were half full, some with only dribbles in them and one or two that were full.

Champ was panting like mad when they got back. But the pallets were safe. Bullet untied him and told him to have a drink. Champ ran up the stairs and into the flat through the open hall door. Bullet never closed it. What would his mother do if she came back one day and found it closed? It was awful to think she might go away again because she couldn't get in.

The boys lined the pallets up along the railings of the flats. They started to lash them with paint. By the time they were finished, the pallets looked like a mural. Every colour of the rainbow was there. They stood back and admired their work, pleased with what they had done.

'I'm starving after that,' Oxo said.

Oxo always thought of his stomach

first. Not that the others weren't hungry. Four hours of slapping on paint had given them an appetite. It was time to go home for dinner.

Oxo and Dizzy went in. Bullet stayed out in the courtyard. He wasn't finished looking at the crazy designs. They changed all the time, depending on where he stood. One part of it looked like a woman's head. He could see the outline of her face – a forehead dipping down into a nose and looping around to make a mouth and a chin. She had a skinny, delicate neck. He thought it might be his mother on the pallets. Perhaps she was sending a message to him. Telling him to finish the ark. Did that mean she was overseas? Or on the far side of a river? He had never been sent a message in this way before.

Five

The boys brought the painted pallets to the canal. They also brought long nails, hammers and ropes to put the ark together. They had the three yellow sheets, some brush handles, two oars and four small wooden barrels they had borrowed from a pub in town. They also had a green leather car seat. Bullet had seen it in a scrap yard and thought it looked lovely. So he borrowed it, not knowing when he would return it. He had decided it would be the captain's seat. Whoever sat in it would be in charge of the vessel. It would, of course, be him who sat there.

Dizzy was in charge of assembly, putting all his DIY knowledge to the test. It went smoothly. The nine pallets were tied together. The barrels were placed in the four corners. The boys tugged the wooden vessel until it hung over the wall of the canal. They lowered it gently, using two ropes, into the water. It went under before it bobbed back up. Then it sat proudly on the surface like a proper sailing ship.

Bullet jumped onto it from the wall and called Champ after him. Oxo and Dizzy, holding an oar each, jumped next. Bullet took up his position in the captain's seat. Champ sat beside him with his head in the air, proud as you like. The ark drifted across the canal towards the wall on the far side.

'Forward,' Bullet commanded, pointing towards the River Liffey in the distance.

Dizzy and Oxo put their oars in the water and started to pull hard. The ark turned in a circle and went nowhere.

'One on either side,' Bullet said. The boys obeyed, just like the good sailors they were. Slowly but surely, they started to make progress. Bullet hopped out of the captain's seat. He took one of the yellow sheets and started to wrap it around one of the upright brush handles they had nailed to the deck. Then he stretched the sheet around a second pole to make a sail. The result was immediate and dramatic. The sail billowed from the wind that moments before had felt like a breeze. The ark, under the wind's power, moved down the canal and out into the river. Their plan was to sail over to the south wall, tie up the ark and take a rest. When they were fed up they would sail back to the north side and dock it for the night. They hadn't planned for nature, however. What felt like a breeze on the canal turned into a gale on the Liffey. Dizzy and Oxo rowed like a couple of madmen. But they couldn't tell the ark where to go. It had a mind all of its own. A third of the way across, they collapsed from their efforts. They were too spent even to talk. They lay there, looking up at the sky, as they drifted down the river.

'I think ...' Oxo said, barely able to form the words. 'I think ... that we ... should ... should ... abandon ship ...'

It was the first sign of panic.

'I can't ... I can't really swim ...' Dizzy said. There was a sadness in his voice.

Bullet stayed in the captain's seat and thought about the *Titanic*. He had seen a programme on TV about it.

'We can't sink. We're safe,' Bullet said.

'We're drifting out to sea and we've no life jackets,' Dizzy said.

'We have Champion,' Bullet said. 'He's better than any life jacket.'

Champ barked his approval. Bullet knew that he could paddle across to the steps and raise the alarm in seconds. He could bark and he could howl in a way that would bring attention faster than a flare in the sky. Dizzy and Oxo weren't so sure. They were heading for the East Link bridge. In no time they would pass under it and out into open sea. Their next stop was Wales.

'My da will kill me if I drown,' Oxo said.

'So will mine,' Dizzy added.

They were close to tears. But Bullet wasn't scared. Dying didn't bother him. Nothing affected him that way since his mother had left. That was the worst thing that could ever happen. No scary thing could compare to it. The truth was he liked being scared because it made him feel alive. His heart beat faster, the way it would if he ever saw her walking down the street again. If he could have her back, even for a second, he wouldn't care if his heart burst out through his chest.

They passed under the East Link and the gale became a hurricane. They were going all over the place, this way and that. The wind came at them from every direction. The yellow sail filled up one way, then another. They had no idea what direction they were going to be blown in next. Bullet jumped up and removed the yellow sheet from the brush handles. Then suddenly, the wind calmed. The ark moved towards a sailing club near the toll bridge. Dozens of boats were moored there. As they drifted in among them, they felt safer and hope returned.

They tied up the ark and climbed onto the jetty nearby. It was a long way home. Oxo and Dizzy were shaking the whole way. They had never imagined sailing could be so dangerous. Bullet, on the other hand, was thrilled. The voyage had given him a taste for adventure. He couldn't wait to see where it would take him next.

Six

Jacko was a parrot who lived in Sammy's Amusement Arcade in town. His home was in a metal cage in an office where the customers got change. He had his own trapeze, like in a circus. He sat there most of the time, looking miserable. People getting change to put in the machines would say, 'Who's a clever girl?' The bird would always reply: 'Jacko's a clever girl. Jacko's a clever girl.' Jacko knew he was male, but he couldn't be bothered. His spirits were very low after being forced to live indoors for so long. He longed for the sun. He wanted open spaces, fresh air, blue skies and trees. Instead he was locked up like a criminal.

'Who's the best boy?' Bullet said. Jacko got excited.

'Jacko's the best boy. Jacko's the best boy,' the parrot answered. He flew down onto the cage front. Bullet knew he could talk to him, but he would have to get up close. He would need to put his nose on Jacko's beak and get in rhythm with his breathing.

'Do you want change?' the cashier asked him. But Bullet didn't hear her because he was looking at Jacko. Jacko's eyes were darting at a hundred miles an hour from wall to wall and ceiling to floor. Bullet knew he was marking out the confines of his cell.

'Do you want change?' the woman asked him again.

Jacko flapped his wings and flew to

the centre of the cage. There he was lit up by a shaft of sunlight coming from the ceiling. It was a skylight. Jacko drank in the attention. Bullet admired his wing span. A stick appeared and jabbed Jacko in the chest, knocking blue and yellow feathers from him.

'Don't do that,' Bullet said.

'And who are you?' the cashier asked him. 'The Prevention of Cruelty to Animals?'

Bullet watched Jacko, who had returned to his trapeze.

'Play the machines or piss off out of here,' the cashier warned Bullet.

Oxo had made five attempts to get a silver watch from a machine. He had come closer with each attempt, fixing his eyes on the same watch each time. It was the one with the diamonds in its own red, satin case. It was all a question of making the arm come across at the right moment. Dizzy egged him on but kept his own money firmly in his pocket. Bullet joined them and watched Oxo try again to catch the watch.

'I nearly had it the last time,' Oxo said.

'He did, he nearly had it,' Dizzy agreed.

'Nearly never won a race,' Bullet said.

'I'll get it this time, watch me,' Oxo said.

'Come on, let's get out of here,' Bullet said.

'One more go, just one more go,' Oxo said.

'We'll be back later, come on,' Bullet said. He marched out of Sammy's Amusement Arcade, followed by the two boys.

★

That night, they returned to rescue Jacko. He was going to be the biggest bird on the ark. So Bullet had decided to make him their mascot. Champ was delighted. He liked big birds. He was dying to meet Jacko. He knew they were going to hit it off. Champ had never met an animal from a warm country. He was curious to find out what they did there.

Bullet put Champ at the front door of the arcade and told him to keep watch. At any sign of trouble he was to let out two barks, followed by a pause and then two more barks. They had practised at home until Champ had it perfect. Bullet climbed up the drainpipe and onto the roof, carefully stepping over the sign that said SAMMY'S AMUSEMENT ARCADE. It was in darkness now, like most of the rest of the city. Dizzy and Oxo followed Bullet onto the flat roof. They made their way across until they found the skylight. Bullet pulled at it. After a few minutes, the catch on the inside snapped and the skylight opened.

It was hard to judge how far down it was to the floor below. In the dark, it looked like an endless black pit. Bullet sat with his feet dangling into empty space. He said he would drop first. Dizzy reached out and took hold of Bullet's arm. Oxo, in turn, held on to Dizzy. They made a human chain. Dizzy lowered Bullet into the black hole. Bullet held on to his hand for dear life. He could hear the trapeze creaking back and forth below him. What if he landed on Jacko's head? He would crush the bird and break his neck.

'Pull me back up,' Bullet ordered.

There was no way Dizzy had the strength to do that. Besides which, Oxo was starting to lose his footing. It was only a matter of seconds before all three of them fell into the hole together.

'I have to let you go,' Dizzy said as Bullet's hand slid from his grasp. Bullet fell through the air. His backside hit the floor with a thud that sent shockwaves up through his body. At least he had missed Jacko. Bullet stood up and faced the bird. He held his hand out very straight. He invited Jacko to perch on his wrist. He was telling the bird that he was the master and would protect him at all times. Jacko flapped his wings and took flight. Then he swooped down and landed softly on Bullet's wrist.

The lads were shouting down for him to look out for a ladder. He ignored them and looked at Jacko. He brought the bird to him so that their noses touched. They exchanged breaths. In no time, Bullet found the bird's rhythm.

'You're safe with me,' Bullet told him. 'I won't ever abandon you.'

'Take me out of this place,' Jacko said. 'It's too cramped.'

'You're coming on the ark with me.'

'That's great. I always wanted to go on an ark.'

The boys on the roof were getting annoyed. Bullet told them to get back down the drainpipe and come round to the front. He opened the main door of the arcade. Champ jumped up on him and licked his face. Oxo and Dizzy rushed in looking for machines to play. None of them was working because the electricity was switched off.

After running round the arcade, they found nothing. They complained to Bullet, who was busy introducing Jacko to Champ.

'We didn't break in to play games,' Bullet said.

'Just one, please,' Oxo said. 'One lousy game, that's all.'

'Once you start, you'll want to play ten,' Bullet said.

'I promise you on my little brother's life, just one go, that's all,' Oxo begged, holding back the tears.

'I think we deserve one game,' Dizzy said in support.

Bullet knew he would never hear the end of it if he refused. He asked Jacko where the switch for the machines was. Jacko flew down and walked into an alcove beside where the cashier sat. Bullet followed him in. There were several switches on a wall. He tried one. Nothing happened. He tried the one next to it. All the emergency signs lit up. He tried two more before the machines kicked into life.

Oxo ran to the machine with the diamond-studded watch. He put a coin in. He released the arm and brought it halfway across. He waited for the watch to come around. He was so excited. He moved the arm as the watch came near. It slid across, missing the target by a quarter of an inch. He kicked the machine as hard as he could. It shook. He kicked it several more times for good measure.

'That machine owes me,' Oxo said, all tensed up.

'You're after putting a fortune into it,' Dizzy said.

Bullet wasted no time training Jacko to sit on his shoulder. It was where he wanted the bird to be. Jacko was safe there. And Bullet could walk around, the captain of all he surveyed. Bullet got ready to leave. Jacko dug his claws into Bullet's shoulder.

'That hurts, I'll have you know,' Bullet said.

'It's supposed to. Why do you think God gave me claws?' Jacko said.

'To get attention, I suppose.'

'Oh, who's a clever captain? Who's a clever captain?'

'I am.'

'Not so clever that you remembered my food. Look on the shelf up there. That's my seed.'

Bullet reached up to get the box when there was an explosion. It ripped through the arcade. Everyone jumped and screamed. Jacko flew up to the safety of his trapeze. Champ ran out the front door onto the street. Bullet covered his ears with his hands and crouched down on the floor. He looked across to see Oxo standing in front of the machine, covered in glass. His face was a maze of little red streams. It was his blood. In one hand he held the diamond-studded watch. In the other was a hammer. He was smiling from ear to ear, delighted with his work in smashing the machine open.

After the loud explosion of the glass, a strange silence took hold. It was as if the other machines had been shouted at by an angry teacher. The sound of a siren could be heard in the distance. It was hard to tell if it was the fire brigade, ambulance or police. Champ barked twice and, after a pause, barked twice again. He ran in from the street and hid behind Bullet. The three boys listened as the siren got nearer and nearer. Bullet put Jacko on his shoulder and they all ran from the arcade. It was bright outside. Without realising, Bullet had turned on the sign on the roof that said Sammy's Amusement Arcade.

Two police cars arrived, one at either end of the street, catching the boys in the middle. Dizzy tried to climb up the drainpipe but was quickly caught. The five suspects, three humans and two animals, were arrested and taken into custody.

Seven

Champ and Jacko were the first to be let go. Jacko was returned to his cage, where he sat on the trapeze and cried for the rest of the night. Champ was taken to Bullet's flat. The handler had to knock twenty-six times before Bullet's father woke from his drunken sleep. He came out to the hall and refused to open the front door.

'I don't own a dog,' he roared.

'We believe it belongs to your son,' the handler said.

'What's wrong with him that he can't look after it himself?'

'He's in custody.'

'What's that?'

'He's up before a judge in the morning. Anti-social behaviour.'

'I knew he'd come to no good.'

Champ tugged at the lead and tried to get away. The handler was taken by surprise and nearly let go. He told the dog to sit and Champ did. Champ looked anything but happy.

'What does the dog look like?' Bullet's father asked.

The handler stared down at Champ.

'To tell you the truth, he looks like three o'clock.'

There was the sound of the door creaking. It opened just enough for a dog to squeeze through. Champ knew he had no option. He made his way in slowly and got an immediate kick in the arse. Then the door closed over again.

'You son is appearing tomorrow. You might want to show up for him.'

★

Bullet, Oxo and Dizzy were brought before Judge Hunt. He loved seeing boys in the dock. It made him feel important. Judge Hunt had met all three boys before. They had appeared before him for non-attendance at school. That time, several years ago, they had barely avoided being sent away. He pretended not to be pleased that they were standing before him again. But he was delighted. He looked over the rim of his glasses at them.

Oxo denied smashing the machine, which was stupid. He was covered in cuts. His fingerprints were all over the hammer. It was obvious he had done it. But he was afraid of being sent away. And that fear drove him to act like he was brain dead.

48

'I'm not going to sit here and listen to these lies, is that understood?' Judge Hunt said. 'Is that understood, young man?'

'Yes, your honour.'

'Did you smash the glass? I want the truth now!'

'I didn't mean to,' Oxo said. 'I only gave it a tap.'

'You smashed the machine, did you not?'

Oxo started to cry. 'Yes, your honour.'

'You smashed the machine and stole a cheap watch.'

'No, your honour.'

'Are you going to stand here and deny it?'

'No, it was a silver watch with diamonds in it.'

'Better still, you stole a diamond-studded watch.'

'I put more than thirty euros into that machine. It owed me.'

'It doesn't matter if you put in a hundred. You're not entitled to smash and grab. I'm not going to stand for it. Do you understand that?'

Oxo could see the gates of Mountjoy Jail opening up to take him in. He couldn't stop the tears. They ran down his face in floods. He tried to show the judge that he had only tapped the glass. He never meant to smash it. He was trying to get his money's worth – that was all. He didn't know the glass was so weak and the hammer was so strong. He hit it too hard. It was an accident. A stupid accident and he was sorry. If the judge let him off he would replace the glass with stuff you couldn't break. He promised that on his little brother's life.

Judge Hunt asked the policeman to put a value on the diamond watch. There was a flurry of activity among the court officials. They went into huddles trying to agree the value of the watch. Bullet kept his gaze firmly on the judge. Bullet thought the judge made himself appear smart by making other people look stupid. Or weak. Judge Hunt was delighted with himself when he made Oxo cry. He was not going to be fooled by an upstart from the inner city.

Word came back that the watch was worth twelve euros and ninety-five cents. The judge sniggered. Oxo realised that the diamonds were fake. He hung his head in shame. He had put enough money into the machine to buy three of the lousy watches.

The judge turned his attention to Bullet. He accused him of the theft of an exotic animal, namely a parrot. He further accused him of putting the animal at serious risk of injury.

'How do you plead?' the judge asked. 'Are you innocent or guilty of the crime?'

Bullet looked round the packed courtroom. There was a man writing in a notebook. Bullet assumed he was from the newspapers. People loved to read about animals being treated badly. A parrot being showered with broken glass was bound to be big news. Bullet was about to become famous as an animal torturer. He couldn't let that happen.

'I would never hurt an animal. They are my friends,' Bullet said. 'If you don't believe me, ask them.'

There was a shocked silence. Everyone stared at Bullet. The solicitor wasn't sure if he was crazy or clever. The man with the notebook turned over a new page and started to write. The judge removed his glasses and wiped them. He put them back on and glared at Bullet.

'Are you making fun of this court, young man?'

'No, your honour.'

'I believe you are. You are making fun at the expense of a poor, dumb animal.'

'Jacko's not dumb. He can speak.'

There was a titter of laughter that spread quickly and became a guffaw. The place was in uproar.

'I think you are trying to make a fool out of me!' the judge shouted. 'You won't succeed. Do you hear me?'

'You can ask Jacko if I hurt him. Bring him here. He'll tell you. He can talk. He's not dumb.'

Everyone was staring at the judge, waiting for his reply. It was common knowledge that parrots could talk. Some of them knew up to fifty words. No one had ever called an animal to speak in court. The judge asked Bullet's solicitor to approach the bench. They whispered back and forth. It was impossible to make out what they were saying. Finally, the solicitor walked across to Bullet in the witness stand.

'If you withdraw this request, the judge will give you the probation act,' the solicitor said.

'What does that mean?' Bullet asked.

'It means you will walk free from this court today.'

'Does that mean I have to say I'm guilty?' Bullet asked. The solicitor looked at Judge Hunt, who smiled. The solicitor looked back at Bullet.

'Yes, you have to plead guilty to the charge.'

'But I didn't hurt Jacko. I'd never hurt him.'

'Just say you're guilty and we'll all get out of here today.'

It was the most important decision of young Bullet's life. A guilty plea would turn him into a torturer in the eyes of the world. He couldn't do that. He didn't care what it cost him. He had to protect his good name.

'I am not guilty,' Bullet said in a strong voice.

'You are a very foolish young man,' the judge said.

'I don't hurt animals. I mind them,' Bullet said.

'You've a funny way of showing it. Breaking into a building and frightening a poor parrot out of its wits.'

'Jacko doesn't like it there.'

'Oh, doesn't he?'

'The noise of the machines frightens him. It's dark and he gets no sun.'

'Maybe he would like it better in St Ultan's.'

'What is St Ultan's?'

'It's a place for young offenders. I'm sending you there for the night. You will appear before me again tomorrow. If you don't change your plea to guilty, I will send you there for twelve months.'

The judge banged his gavel. Everyone in the courtroom stood up. Bullet was handcuffed and taken to St Ultan's. But all he could think about was Jacko and Champ. The three of them, he thought, would all spend the night in prisons, separated from one another but united.

Eight

Bullet didn't like St Ultan's. If he was sent away there, he would never see anyone again. No bus came near it. It was the back of beyond. The boys in there were older than him. Everyone was in a gang. Some boys had scars and others had tattoos. The food was horrible: lumpy porridge, toast that was rock hard and cold tea. He had no desire to return there, none at all.

He decided to change his plea. What did it matter if he said guilty when he knew in his heart that he was innocent?

It was only words. One word. Guilty. He could say it and then, under his breath, he could say 'not'. If God was listening, and he was sure He would be, He'd know Bullet was innocent.

The courtroom was packed. The reporter with the notebook waved at Bullet. Beside him were three more reporters, all female, with their pens at the ready. There were people from the flats sitting on the benches. Some of them waved. Some gave him the thumbs-up. He spotted a familiar face among the crowd. It took him a moment to realise it was Mr Barrett from next door. He hadn't seen him in over a year. Mr Barrett smiled at him and nodded his head.

Dizzy and Oxo were in the front row with their parents. They were all cleaned up. It was the first time Bullet had seen them in suits and ties since their Confirmation day, three years ago. Dizzy had a newspaper in his hand. He turned it around and showed it to Bullet. It was the *Evening Herald* from the night before. Across it was a banner headline: BOY CALLS PARROT TO TESTIFY.

'You were all over the papers,' Oxo said, trying to hide his excitement but failing.

'People were ringing in to the radio about you,' Dizzy said.

'What were they saying?' Bullet asked him.

'Some people said they should lock you up and throw the key away,' Oxo said.

'Don't mind him,' Dizzy said. 'Most people said you were a hero.'

Bullet saw his solicitor. He was talking to a woman. The woman was using her hands a great deal. Bullet could see her hair but not her face. It was black and curly, just like his ma's in the photograph. The solicitor moved away and the woman looked at Bullet. Straight into his eyes. It was his ma. No mistake – his ma. He hadn't seen her for four hundred and thirty-two days. He wanted to scream at her for leaving him on his own all that time. He wanted to hug her, too, and melt into her until he felt safe. He wanted her to run over to him and put her arms around him and bury the past.

Judge Hunt entered and everyone stood. In that moment, Bullet's ma walked over to her son and hugged him.

'I'm sorry, son,' she whispered in his ear.

'It's all right, Ma,' he whispered back.

The judge sat and someone shouted, 'This court is in session.' Bullet's solicitor came over and touched Bullet and his ma on the shoulder. They hugged for a few more seconds. They separated and Bullet's ma wiped her eyes with the back of her sleeve.

'I gave you a day to consider your position,' the judge said. 'So how do you plead?'

Bullet had been practising the moment all morning. Head bowed and in a defeated voice he would say, 'Guilty.' But his head wasn't bowed. He was standing up straight with his chest out. He had his mother beside him. His courage had brought her back. She had read about him in the papers and had come to be with him in his hour of need. He had nothing to fear from anyone.

'I plead not guilty, your honour.'

The judge wrote something in his trial book. The solicitor called Helen Ferguson as his first witness. Bullet's ma took the stand. She faced the judge and told him about her relationship with her son.

'I wish I could say I've been a good mother, but I can't. I failed my son, your honour. I left home to get away from his father. I should have taken Daniel with me, but I didn't. That was a mistake and I'm going to pay for it for the rest of my life.'

When questioned by the solicitor, she told of her troubled marriage and home life. It was a story of fear and violence. She got upset recalling how she would pretend to Daniel that she had fallen down the stairs and broken her arm. In reality, she had been pushed. Yet her husband never laid a finger on her son, or not as far as she knew. In the end, she feared for her life and fled. She was ashamed that she had abandoned her son. She turned around to him from the witness box and asked his forgiveness.

'I am so sorry I left you. Please forgive me.'

'It's all right, Ma, honest.'

At that point, the judge reminded Helen Ferguson that she was in a court of law.

'You're accusing my son of torturing an animal.'

'He was caught in the act of stealing a parrot. That's cruelty to an animal.'

'What I did to my son is much more cruel.'

'That may be, but you are not on trial.'

'Daniel has a disabled dog. His name is Champion. He only has one eye.'

'That has nothing to do with this case, Mrs Ferguson.'

'He loves that dog. He'd kill anyone who tried to harm him.'

Oxo jumped to his feet and put his hand in the air, like he was in school. 'Bullet talks to him, your honour. Champ understands everything he says,' Oxo said.

The judge told Oxo to sit down.

'You're worried that my son was cruel to the parrot, am I right?' asked Bullet's ma.

'I'm concerned about all cruelty to animals,' said Judge Hunt.

'If you take Daniel away from Champion, is that not cruelty to a dog?'

A round of applause broke out in the courtroom. Bullet looked at his mother. He was so proud that she had stood up for him. The solicitor told Judge Hunt that he had over twenty witnesses who would say similar things about the accused. But it wasn't deemed necessary. The hearing lasted less than half an hour. Bullet was bound to the peace and ordered to stay away from Sammy's Amusement Arcade. The important thing was that the charges against him were dropped. No one could ever point the finger at him and say that he had tortured an animal.

Nine

In the days that followed, Bullet pieced together the jigsaw of the past. His mother had run away with Mr Barrett and was living with him in Cork. He was sure the fight between Princess and Champ had something to do with this. He asked Champ to tell him the truth.

'Who started the fight with Princess?' he asked.

'I did,' Champ said straight off.

'I'm disappointed in you,' Bullet said. 'I thought I could trust you.'

'You can trust me.'

'I can't if you lie to me,' Bullet said. He turned away from Champ in disgust.

'I fought Princess for you,' Champ said. Bullet turned back to him.

'I fought her for the family honour. I didn't want to, but your father said I had to. It was his only way of getting back at Mr Barrett.'

'Why did you listen to him?'

'He said he'd drown me in the canal if I didn't obey.'

Bullet's father had once threatened him with the same fate. It happened the first time Bullet was up in court, when he appeared before Judge Hunt for missing school. Bullet went to school every day for six months after that. He went in fear of his life. He understood how Champ must have felt when Bullet's dad told him to take on the fight that would cost him his eye.

Bullet felt very sorry for Champ and very cross at his father. Only for his dad's stupidity, Champ would still have the use of both his eyes.

'No more lies then, is that a promise?' Bullet said.

'I promise. Paws crossed and tail between the legs,' Champ said and meant it.

'I promise, too,' Bullet said.

'What do you promise?' Champ asked.

'No more lies from this out,' Bullet said.

'You didn't lie. It was me who lied,' Champ reminded him.

Bullet had that look on his face, guilt with a hint of pride.

'You lied too. Is that what you're saying?' Champ said. 'I can see it in your face. Out with it. Out with the lies.'

'Well, you know I said that Princess was dead.'

'Yes, you did. I remember.'

'Well, she's not dead. She's very much alive, in fact. She lives with my ma and Mr Barrett in Cork.'

'Cork is two hundred miles away. Good luck to her.'

'The thing is, we're going down to stay with them. For a month. And you're sharing a room with Princess, I'm afraid.'

Champ went mad, running around in circles after his tail. He did that when he was frustrated. Bullet knew he shouldn't laugh, but he couldn't stop himself. Why did Champ run after his tail when he knew he couldn't catch it? It was pathetic and it was funny.

In the end, they went to Cork, but only after they were told Champ could sleep with Bullet. The first night there, Bullet brought Champ and Princess together and made the peace. It was very emotional, seeing them make up, especially when Princess stroked the socket of Champ's missing eye with her paw. It was a nice way for the cat to make amends. Champ licked under her chin with his tongue. Princess got a fit of the giggles. Then she collapsed in a heap and Bullet and Champ nearly burst their sides. She was so funny. It was a happy ending to a conflict in which they were both innocent.

Bullet and Champ had the best holiday ever on the farm. Four weeks of doing country things: milking cows, collecting eggs and making soda bread. When Bullet arrived back in Dublin, he gave Oxo and Dizzy a pot of jam each. It was made out of blackberries he had collected from a hedge at the back of his ma's house.

'Do you want to see Jacko?' Oxo said.

Bullet's eyes lit up and, just as quickly, lost their sparkle again. He was barred from going into Sammy's for as long as he lived. It was part of the court order.

'He's not in the arcade any more,' Oxo said. 'Do you know where he is?'

Bullet looked interested but confused.

'He's in Dublin Zoo,' Oxo said.

'The men came and took him out of the arcade,' Dizzy added.

'Shut up, you. I'm telling him. The men from the Cruelty to Animals took him,' Oxo went on. 'They put him in the bird house in Dublin Zoo.'

'Why didn't you tell me this before now?' Bullet said.

*

That afternoon, Bullet brought Champ to the zoo. They went through the usual routine. Champ jumped in over the turnstile. Bullet screamed after him to come back. The louder he screamed, the faster Champ ran to get away from him.

'Mister, can I get my dog back?' Bullet begged the doorman through tear-filled eyes. It worked every time. They would avoid each other inside and meet up at Pets Corner when it was time to go home.

Jacko was perched on a tree. He couldn't believe it when he saw Bullet. He flew up into the air above him, then dived down and landed on his shoulder with a great squawk. The bird looked beautiful. His feathers were shining. He had lost quite a bit of weight. Jacko told him about being freed from his cage in the arcade.

'What's happening with the ark?' Jacko wanted to know. 'Are we still on for a trip on it?'

'It's moored down at the bridge. I was thinking of taking it out into the bay and heading for one of the islands.

Lambay or Ireland's Eye, maybe,' Bullet said.

'Who's a clever captain? Who's a clever captain?'

It was non-stop chat all the way. In no time, darkness seemed to have fallen and the zoo had emptied.

'How is Champ? Is he behaving himself?' Jacko asked.

Bullet had forgotten him. In the effort to catch up with Jacko's news, it had slipped his mind to meet Champ at Pets Corner. He ran off at double speed, but Champ wasn't there. Then he saw Champ coming with the lion keeper.

'I found him at the front gate. He was crying for you. He figured he was abandoned, I think,' said the lion keeper.

Bullet got down on his knees and scratched Champ under the chin. 'He knows he wasn't abandoned, don't you, Champ?'

Champ barked twice. The lion keeper was impressed.

'I'd never abandon you – not now, not ever.'

Champ barked twice again. The lion keeper headed off. When he was out of earshot, Champ jumped up on Bullet and bared his teeth in anger. 'I was two hours waiting at Pets Corner! What the hell kept you?'

Champ was angry the whole way home. He had managed to get the two of them into the zoo and had then been ignored. He had wanted to spend time with Jacko, too. He loved exotic birds. It wasn't fair. Bullet could go on his own in future and pay his way into the zoo like everybody else.

Back home, Bullet hid two biscuits behind his back. It was the oldest trick in the book. Champ wasn't going to fall for it. He wasn't going to beg. He was simply going to ignore Bullet. Except the drool was hanging out of his mouth. And his stomach felt very empty. He was a dog and it was natural for him to beg.

'Come on, I won't tease you,' Bullet said. He held out the biscuits. 'In fact, I'll tell you a story.'

'What kind of a story?'

'A true story about Bullet and Champ and Jacko and the ark.'

'What about Oxo and Dizzy?'

'Oxo and Dizzy, too.'

Champ sniffed the air. The smell of biscuit was everywhere. But it was the promise of the story that did the trick. He scoffed the bone-shaped biscuits and settled down in front of Bullet on the rug. This was going to be a true story. Champ preferred those. They were much better than the ones that started 'once upon a time'. They were for kids, and he wasn't a kid. He was a dog.

OPEN DOOR SERIES

Sad Song by Vincent Banville
In High Germany by Dermot Bolger
Not Just for Christmas by Roddy Doyle
Maggie's Story by Sheila O'Flanagan
Jesus and Billy Are Off to Barcelona
by Deirdre Purcell
Ripples by Patricia Scanlan

No Dress Rehearsal by Marian Keyes
Joe's Wedding by Gareth O'Callaghan
The Comedian by Joseph O'Connor
Second Chance by Patricia Scanlan
Pipe Dreams by Anne Schulman
Old Money, New Money by Peter Sheridan

An Accident Waiting to Happen
by Vincent Banville
The Builders by Maeve Binchy
Letter from Chicago by Cathy Kelly
Driving with Daisy by Tom Nestor
It All Adds Up by Margaret Neylon
Has Anyone Here Seen Larry?
by Deirdre Purcell

The Story of Joe Brown by Rose Doyle
Stray Dog by Gareth O'Callaghan
The Smoking Room by Julie Parsons
World Cup Diary by Niall Quinn
Fair-Weather Friend by Patricia Scanlan
The Quiz Master by Michael Scott

Mrs Whippy by Cecelia Ahern
The Underbury Witches by John Connolly
Mad Weekend by Roddy Doyle
Not a Star by Nick Hornby
Secrets by Patricia Scanlan
Behind Closed Doors by Sarah Webb

Lighthouse by Chris Binchy
The Second Child by John Boyne
Three's a Crowd by Sheila O'Flanagan
Bullet and the Ark by Peter Sheridan
An Angel at My Back by Mary Stanley
Star Gazing by Kate Thompson